MW00952322

Life's Dueling Dualities

A GRANDFATHER'S LEGACY OF WISDOM

Stephen Michael Soreff, MD

Copyright © 2019 Stephen Michael Soreff, MD
All rights reserved
First Edition

PAGE PUBLISHING, INC.
Conneaut Lake, PA

First originally published by Page Publishing 2019

ISBN 978-1-64544-897-6 (pbk)
ISBN 978-1-64544-898-3 (digital)

Printed in the United States of America

To my parents, Louis Soreff, MD, and Rebecca Zoken Soreff, who gave me the love of learning and the tools to pursue it; and to my sister, Linda Soreff Siegel, who spread that love into many generations.

INTRODUCTION

One faces the future with one's past.
                                    —Pearl S. Buck

Welcome, grandsons Westley and Foster, and everyone else. As a psychiatrist, a grandfather, a father, a partner to Peggy, a son, a brother, a wannabe golfer, a jogger, a sailor, and a hiker, I have learned a great deal. In my journey as an engaged participant, a veteran of the School of Hard Knocks, and a survivor of making many mistakes, I have discovered life's essential but contradictory messages. I am writing this book so I can share my insights with you. However, before I get to tell you them, I want to acquaint you this volume's unique literary style.

The uniqueness starts here. "She was only a bootlegger's daughter, but they loved her still." Some folks may groan knowingly at that joke, others will gape at its incongruity, and some will be offended by it—sorry. Most of my college class will not get it. To the point, a still is a device to make alcohol, a.k.a. moonshine, by people known as bootleggers. The reason for that tale is that I have *distilled* all my life's experiences, insights, thoughts, and I hope, wisdom, into this book.

Cutting to the chase, I have discovered life is composed of six dual messages and one transcendent notion. The first message involves either doing it right now or thinking about it—carpe diem versus contemplation. Remember, the early bird may get the worm, but the second mouse gets the cheese. The second identifies ambivalence as the key to understanding all relationships. Ambivalence means simultaneously both loving and hating someone or something. As one of my colleagues once said about his wife, "Divorce, *never*, but homicide, maybe." The third one embraces the classic predicament of the heart versus the head. This is often portrayed as right brain versus left brain, or men are from Mars and women from Venus, or emotion and passion versus thinking and logic. In Hollywood movies, the heart wins.

The fourth explores whether to work alone or as part of a group; to pursue activities solo, as an individual achievement, or to be part of a team, with its collective genius. Baseball offers an example of both. A player can win the game, but in reality, the team takes the series. The fifth presents the dilemma of whether to follow the rules or to go on your own initiative. A NASA astronaut once said that, in some situations, adhering to NASA procedures saved lives, yet at other times, breaking them saved lives. And the sixth focuses on striving for a one big goal yet also paying attention to the immediate objective or to everyday realities. For example, you may want to write the great American novel, but you need to earn money to pay the rent.

Steve with grandsons left Foster and right Westley

Although life can be looked at through the lens of these six dueling, contradictory messages, they themselves are incomplete and insufficient to cover all situations. The answer lies in how one can transcend these quandaries. Transcendence is the book's last chapter.

My hope for this book is that it can be viewed in two metaphorical representations. The first image can be seen as "That's one small step for man, one giant leap for mankind." Perhaps a bit grandiose, but so am I. The value of this volume is not only for my grandchildren but also for everyone. Yes, you too! To the reader, please note the YouTube reference. My second vision for this book is that it will join the ranks of Rudyard Kipling's "If (You'll Be a Man, My Son)" and the Earl of Chesterfield Philip Dormer Stanhope's letters, written by Lord Chesterfield to his son. Or, at least, you will find it entertaining, clever, and useful.

So join me as I spin the threads of these seven chapters into the fabric of an understanding of your lives. And through an appreciation of these dueling dual messages and the transcendental conclusion, you all will make better life decisions.

CHAPTER 1

Carpe Diem versus Reflection and Contemplation

In reply to the warning "Torpedoes ahead!" given by a ship ahead, Admiral Farragut called out, "Damn the torpedoes...full speed!" and taking the lead with his flagship, the Hartford, sailed over the double row of mines and into Mobile Bay in Alabama (Farragut).

"The ultimate value of life depends upon awareness and the power of *contemplation* rather than upon mere survival" (Aristotle).

Everyone will confront situations where you must either do something right now or ponder on the alternatives. There is a super computer game in the store you want. It is on sale for just that week. You really, really want it. If you do not act on it *now*, it will revert to a higher price, or even worse, it might not be there in the future. So you buy it! That sounds so simple and makes much sense. Yet there is the alternative. You resist the urge, and instead, you go home and look it up online. There, you discover that the game is being discontinued because of a flaw in its design. Your restraint paid off.

Two Carpe Diem Military Examples from the Civil War

History provides many incidences when *carpe diem* carried the day. Spoiler alert! In the literary accounts, action is depicted often more spectacular and is more lauded than moments of quiet deliberation and contemplation.

At Gettysburg

Let us go back to the climactic Civil War's Battle of Gettysburg, July1–3, 1863. General Robert E. Lee, with his army of Northern Virginia, has invaded the Union State of Pennsylvania. His troops had gained an early advantage on the first day by moving into the town of Gettysburg. On the second day, they had nearly taken a hill, called Little Round Top, adjacent to Cemetery Ridge. That flank knoll protected the entire Union Army's position on Cemetery Ridge. It held the key to the whole battle at that moment.

The Confederate infantry, numbering about a thousand, continuously assaulted the hill. Joshua Chamberlain commanded the high ground with 308 soldiers of the twentieth Maine Volunteer Infantry and had control of Little Round Top. But as the battle progressed, Chamberlain's troops ran out of ammunition. The Confederate soldiers were about to take the hill. The Union's entire line was about to be exposed and threatened. It was a desperate situation.

Chamberlain ordered his line to fix bayonets and to attack down Little Round Top. It proved to be a brilliant maneuver. He had seized the moment and turned defeat into a key victory. The Confederate ranks split and ran. The now attacking Union troops captured four hundred of the fleeing Confederate infantry.

In Mobile Bay

Again, from the American Civil War, comes another example of seizing the moment. In this case, the Union's Admiral David Farragut was leading his fleet to attack the Confederate's naval base at Mobile Bay in the state of Alabama. That was on August 5, 1864. The first ship advancing into the harbor signed that there were "Torpedoes Ahead." In response to the immediate danger, Admiral Farragut issued forth from his flagship Hartford, "Damn the torpedoes," and proceeded dramatically into the Confederate port. His armada passed over the mines without incident, defeated the Confederate fleet, and gained the victory. Yes, once again, decisive action carried the day.

Statue of Admiral David Farragut

A Contemplation Military Example from the Crimean War

Lest you come away feeling that swift action always succeeds, let me show you the opposite result. In the Crimean War, England invaded Russia. At the Battle of Balaclava, as part of the Siege of Sevastopol (1854–1855), Major General, the Earl of Cardigan, ordered his British light cavalry of 673 soldiers to attack a distant Russian position. That was on October 25, 1854. To reach Russian emplacement, his troops had to pass through a valley flanked by the Fedyukhin Heights and the Causeway Heights. Russian forces commanded these heights and raked fire down upon the advancing cavalry. Alfred, Lord Tennyson's poem "The Charge of the Light Brigade" depicts what then happened.

> Cannon to right of them,
> Cannon to left of them,

Cannon in front of them
Volley'd and thunder'd;
Storm'd at with shot and shell,
Boldly they rode and well,
Into the jaws of Death,
Into the mouth of Hell
Rode the six hundred…

Then they rode back, but not
Not the six hundred…

On that day, less than two hundred of the cavalry returned from the "Valley of Death." Had the general used reconnaissance, better intelligence, and more careful deliberation, the outcome could have been quite different, and the huge death toll perhaps could have been avoided.

Carpe Diem in Other Actions

Thus far, I have dwelt only with military examples of *Carpe Diem*. Now let me provide a maritime example. On the night of February 18 and 19, 1952, two—let me repeat that for emphasis—two different tankers broke apart midship in the powerful Nor'easter off Cape Cod, Massachusetts. Michael Tougias and Casey Sherman, in their gripping chronicle of the amazing rescues by the United States Coast Guard *The Finest Hours*, tells a dramatic story of the importance of timing. One tanker called the Mercer had suffered a disastrous break in the middle of the ship and split in half. Many crew members were trapped in the stern section. Captain John Joseph, in command of the Coast Guard cutter Acushnet, had to maneuver his ship next to the stricken stern of the Mercer. The waves were as high as seventy feet. He guided his vessel parallel to the stern. Then, depending on the waves' action, the gap between the Mercer's fantail and the Acushnet's deck ranged from a few feet to several stories. The terrified, trapped crew had to time their individual leaps when that distance between the two ships' decks was closest. All eighteen sailors made the leap without one casualty.

Carpe Diem Versus Reflection and Contemplation in Music and Literature

Carpe Diem in Music

Decisive action need not be limited to the field of battle or great nautical feats. It also occurs in the world of music. "Silent Night" was written on a night when the plans for music were disrupted by a broken organ in the new church. By popular legend, Father Joseph Mohr composed "Silent Night" in one night. It came about because the organ was at the Church of St. Nicholas in Oberndorf, Austria, was broken. He needed a song that did not require an organ. So on December 24, 1818, he wrote that classic Christmas song.

Contemplation in Music

However, lest you think that *carpe diem* is the only way music is composed, let us look at the Dvořák's "New World Symphony." He commenced work on it in the fall of 1892 and completed it in May of 1893. In that masterpiece, he synthesized American Negro spirituals with native American music, as well as incorporating his travel impressions about the United States. It was a work of contemplation and thoughtfulness, and it demonstrated the value of taking your time.

In Literature

Aesop's Fable

Perhaps another way to illustrate the choices between seizing the day or reflecting upon the options is to look at one of Aesop's fables called "The Sun and the Wind." Aesop, a slave in early Greek history, has had a number of stories attributed to him. These provided neat moral messages. In this fable, the Wind and the Sun decide to see which is the more powerful. They select a man wearing a coat. They would then compete to prove which of the two can make him take off his coat. First, the wind blows mightier which only serves to make the man pull his coat closer to him. Next, the Sun takes its time and shines gently upon him, and upon which, the man removes his coat. The classic moral interpretation of this story is that gentle persuasion is better than brute force. And my purpose of telling this story is that it shows that taking time rather than just doing something can be more effective.

Carpe Diem Versus Reflection and Contemplation in the Famous Marshmallow Experiment

Perhaps, to be more concrete and abstract at the same time, let me describe the famous marshmallow experiment. It offers another way of looking merits at immediacy versus patience. This was a classic experiment conducted at Stanford University in the early 1960s. An experimenter, Walter Mischel, along with his graduate students, presented nursery school students with a marshmallow. Each student was alone in a room and was told one could eat the marshmallow now, or if one waited for approximately fifteen minutes and did not eat the first marshmallow, then the student would get a second marshmallow. What did they do, take the immediate one or hold out for the extra one? By the way, watching the videos of children deliberating whether to eat the marshmallow or not are hilarious (Urist 2017).

What made that experiment so particularly interesting and often cited is that the researchers followed the children for a number of years afterwards. They discovered the children who did not immediately eat their marshmallow and waited, did better on their SAT (Scholastic Aptitude Test) scores and have a lower BMI (body mass index) than those who ate the first marshmallow. Maybe there is some virtue in waiting?

Looking Ahead Carpe Diem Quotes

Well, Westley and Foster, where are we right now? The first set of contradictions deals with whether to act or think about it. There is the old chestnut, "Do not engage mouth until brain is in gear." This turns out to be one of the few admonitions where contemplation trumps action. Movies feature decisive dramatic actions rather than either a chess or bridge game. And what follows is a brief rump through the quotation world of one-liners, which lionizes doing rather than thinking. Here are some examples.

> As you grow older, you'll find the only things you regret are the things you didn't do. (Zachary Scott)

> You may delay, but time will not. (Benjamin Franklin)

> Enjoy yourself. It's later than you think. (Chinese Proverb)

> Contemplation often makes life miserable. We should act more, think less, and stop watching ourselves live. (Nicolas de Chamfort)

> If you were going to die soon and had only one phone call you could make, who would you call

and what would you say? And why are you wait-ing? (Stephen Levine)

Only that day dawns to which we are awake. (Henry David Thoreau)

Every second is of infinite value. (Johann Wolfgang von Goethe)

Later never exists. (Unknown)

Carpe diem. (Horace)

Live every day as if it were your last and then some day you'll be right. (H. H. "Breaker" Morant)

So you see, or better, you can hear the sages opt of action. But you must take your own counsel and make your decision.

The Words and Worlds of Contradictions

We live in a world of contradictions. Brandon Specktor's *Idioms for the Indecisive* highlights the differences, contradictions, and conflicts.

1. He who hesitates is lost. But Haste makes waste. 2. Opportunity never knocks twice. But Look before you leap. 3. Out of sight, out of mind, but absence makes the heart grow fonder. 4. The pen is mightier than the sword, but actions speak louder than words. 5. What you see is what you get, but don't judge a book by its cover. 6. Birds of a feather flock together, but opposites attract. 7. Many hands make light work, but too many cooks spoil the broth. 8. Practice makes perfect, but nothing is perfect.

9. Live life every moment, but plan and save for the future. 10. God is dead, but there are no atheists in a foxhole. 11. The glass is half-full, but the class is half-empty. 12. Or as I said before, the early bird gets the worm, but the second mouse gets the cheese.

A Snowstorm Offers Another Example

My snowshoed path

However, in a recent week, I did practice what I preach, or better said, talked about. We have had very snowy blizzard-filled winter in New Hampshire, in fact, in all New England. Perhaps, someday you'll see T-shirts saying I survived the winter of 2015. So on Washington's birthday, now combined into the holiday of Presidents' Day, I had the opportunity to stay home, with no college classes to teach, because of a snowstorm. Yes, I did have students' works to check. And oh, yes, I had snow to shovel. However, the sun that afternoon danced around the lake. The deep brilliantly shining snow beckoned me. So I went out snowshoeing. I broke trail; I followed other trails. I made it across to Seaman's Road on the trail I call the Northwest Passage. It was great. I felt the wind. I went into deep snow. I did seize the day and felt better for it. In turn, when I resumed my tasks, I did so with renewed energy and enthusiasm.

A Lesson from a College Reunion

Steve at his 50th Tufts College Reunion

Ready, for a brief but neat digression? This deals with a variant of the *carpe diem* theme. In the spring of 2014, I attended my Tufts College class's fiftieth reunion. One of the events during that weekend celebration was a workshop group I ran entitled "How to Keep Mentally Healthy with Aging." Classmates offered their wisdom about aging. However, one of the School of Engineering graduates provided the best idea. His motto was, "It is better to finish than be perfect." By reaching fifty years from college, we all appreciated that our careers, our lives, our families, and our experiences were good but not perfect. The Nike motto proclaimed, "Just do it." Yes, start it, and stay with it; that is what's important. The maxim of that day was "completed, not perfect."

A Baseball Paradox

To belabor the theme and the dilemma, let me highlight it with two examples from the world of baseball. Two baseball movies illustrate this dueling duality. In the 1988 film, *Bull Durham*, one of the characters says, "Don't think, just throw." Again, just do it! Right? Yet in the 1999 movie, *For Love of the Game*, one character utters, "Think, Billy. Don't just throw." (Bathroom Readers)

A Heartfelt Example

Well, to get more personal, dramatic, and immediate, let me tell you a true recent story. I was attending an evening fundraiser concert held by my online local newspaper, *the Forum*. In the middle of the last act before the intermission, the fiddle player suddenly dropped to the floor. Many of us rushed to his aid. Although he was breathing, when I took his pulse, he did not have one. Meanwhile, someone ran and got an automated external defibrillator (AED) machine.

The AED machine, which is also a heart monitor, once the electrodes were in placed on his chest and once it was turned on, announced, "Heart not working." Then it said, "Stay clear of the patient, and administer a shock." Someone pressed the button. The machine delivered an electrical charge. His body jumped, and his heart started. Amazingly, quick thinking, having the right equipment, and knowledgeable folk saved his life; *carpe diem* saved him.

Since luck played a such a role there too, (he had the cardiac event at the right time and place), I want to add another story. Victor Frankl, in his classic work, *Man's Search for Meaning*, talked about luck. It occurred during the time just before his concentration camp was liberated. He stayed behind to help several of the sick inmates. Meanwhile, the Nazi guards were transporting his fellow prisoners to another camp. He later found out that the prisoners whom were supposedly to be taken to another camp were instead killed by the Nazi officers.

What about Procrastination?

A quick detour discussion of one the words I hate the most, "procrastination." I see it all the time in the college students' term papers. Every semester, I urge my pupils to pick a topic for their papers. That alone is a difficult task. I want them to select *their* subject rather than me telling them one. And by making their choice in advance this permitted them to use the library and gain the required journal references instead of the unallowed website sources.

By their early selection, they can work on the paper throughout the semester. But it is much more my wish than their reality. Ultimately, they do their term papers the night before. Their grades on the papers reflect their procrastination.

Same theme with a twist. I believe one should not put off to tomorrow what you can do today. When I practiced emergency psychiatry in a general hospital's emergency department, I would always write my chart note right after I had seen the patient. By doing that, I avoided the danger of later not remembering, and therefore, not recording critical information. And I was then ready to attend to the next emergency patient's arrival. This was my small victory over procrastination.

The Mystic Experience

Westley and Foster
at Mystic Seaport

Foster at Mystic Seaport

Actually, Westley and Foster, I saw this dilemma play out on our recent trip to Mystic Seaport, The Museum of America and the Sea in Mystic, Connecticut. Your parents asked you two to choose between playing for a few more minutes at the children's room or go to the gift shop later. You gave up the children's room and metaphorically do not eat the marshmallow. And you selected the gift shop. And I was glad to buy things for you, thereby fulfilling the role of a grandparent—to spoil the grandchildren.

Conclusion

In the end, each of you will discover that sometimes quick, decisive action can win a battle and save a life, or a more deliberative approach might defeat the enemy and save lives. So, it depends on you and the situation. This is not profound but realistic. Good luck.

References

Aristotle. https://www.brainyquote.com/quotes/aristotle_132267. Accessed 3/20/18.

Bathroom Readers' Institute, Uncle John's Bathroom Reader Takes a Swing at Baseball, 2008, Bathroom Readers' Press, Ashland, Oregon.

Farragut http://www.americaslibrary.gov/jb/civil/jb_civil_ftmorgan_2.html accessed 3/20/18.

Frankl, VE, Man's Search for Meaning Third Edition, New York, Simon & Schuster, 1984.

Michael Tougias and Casey Sherman, The Finest Hours The True Story of the U.S. Coast Guard's Most Daring Sea Rescue., New York, Scribner, 2009.

Tennyson, *The Charge of the Light Brigade,* https://www.poetryfoundation.org/poems/45319/the-charge-of-the-light-brigade, accessed 12/7/18.

STEPHEN MICHAEL SOREFF, MD

Specktor, B., "Idioms for the Indecisive," Readers' Digest, Nov. 2016, pp 118.

Urist, Jacoba., What the Marshmallow Test Really Teaches About Self-Control, http://www.theatlantic.com/health/archive/2014/09/what-the-marshmallow-test-really-teaches-about-self-control/380673/, accessed 2/18/17.

CHAPTER 2

Ambivalence

Reflection on Pawtuckaway Lake

It seems we are capable of immense love and loyalty, and as capable of deceit and atrocity. It's probably this shocking ambivalence that makes us unique.

—John Scott

Our step next to make good decisions is to appreciate the complex and profound idea called ambivalence. It is often misunderstood. And yet it is the key to all relationships

Let me call on Westley and Foster to illustrate this concept. Your mother says you have to go to bed. You want to stay up and play. She says, "No, bedtime!" At that instant, you are annoyed with her, but you also love her. In the end, you give her a hug and a kiss as she puts you into bed, the very bed you do not want to go to! So you might say that, at that moment, you experience mixed feelings toward your mother. Yes, of course, you love her. Just see how you feel when she leaves you alone for too long. You really miss her. So agreed; you love her! But when she tells you, without room for negotiation, "You must go to bed," you really do dislike her. Yet you still love her! Welcome to the world of ambivalence.

Time to see the official definition of ambivalence. Ambivalence means having two diametrically opposed emotions at the same time. That seems so impossible. That is amazing and so unreal but also very valid. Remember how you felt about your mother telling you to go to bed? At that moment, you had a taste of it.

Ambivalence forms the basis of many jokes. How would you feel when your mother-in-law drives your beloved 1975 Cadillac convertible off a cliff? Here is the translation for you, kids. Husbands are supposed to not hold their mother-in-laws in high esteem. Thus, they should be "happy" when they are not around. But they also love their cars, especially if their vehicles are vintage Cadillac convertibles. Another example, as previously cited, is something my colleague once said about his wife. "Divorce, *never*, but homicide, maybe."

So accepting that the term ambivalence is almost counterintuitive, let's see how this can apply to your everyday life. You're in school now. (Oh my, you are growing up!) Students love to complain about being there, and at the same time, they actually enjoy it. The same students who cannot wait until recess often are the ones who are bored during the long summer vacation and are anxious to get back to classes in the fall.

Here is another example of ambivalence involving teasing. Some people both love and hate to be teased at the same time. There is the classic scenario of the little girl in the playground. First, she pokes fun at a boy. He acts annoyed, but at the same time, he appreciates her attention. He responds to the "attack" by running after the little girl. She screams and runs away. She feels pursued. If she gets too far ahead of the chasing lad, she slows down. She wants him to pursue him but not quite catch her. They are playing, and they are demonstrating mutual affection and annoyance.

Here is yet another example of ambivalence. People, every day, talk about taxes and municipal services. Citizens complain about taxes all the time; they resent paying them, and they note that their taxes are too high. But they also demand government services. Although they grumble that the police respond too slowly, they complain that the school is not doing its job of educating children, and they are annoyed about the library's hours. But, they still want and demand those very same services. And they do pay their taxes.

A Nottingham, New Hampshire stone wall

Perhaps the New England poet, Robert Frost, caught the ambivalent feelings about the stone walls when he wrote in his famous poem "Mending Walls." It began with "Something there is that doesn't love a wall" and ends with "Good fences make good neighbors." Warning! Digression ahead. When I went to Tufts College, Medford, Massachusetts (class of 1964), I got to see and hear Robert Frost in person. He came on campus, and he recited poetry in Cohen Auditorium. Frost stood there, as if in a country store in front of an iron woodstove and recited, "The Death of the Hired Man" by heart.

Confession time! I am ambivalent about writing. Yes, I love to produce written material, and I especially am thrilled when it gets published. But at the same time, sitting down to write is quite difficult for me to do. I play computer games, like Snood, in order to avoid actually writing. More recently, I find playing card games, like Hearts and Cribbage on the computer, as pleasant diversion. I think about what I am going to write, then I just have trouble where the rubber meets the road. I love and hate writing, but I keep on writing.

I want to wander into a variation on the theme of ambivalence. In a nutshell, which is more important, people or places? I recall, years ago, seeing a movie in which a British soldier recounts something like this (please, read this with a British accent), "I've been around the world from Suez to Singapore, from Rio de Janeiro to New York. But to tell you the truth, mates, what really matters is the people there." Yes, that's it. The folks you meet along the way are much more important than the places that you visit.

I had this realization about the importance of people. In July 2012, Peggy and I, along with family and friends, took a once-in-a-lifetime inside-passage cruise-ship vacation to Alaska and British Columbia. We visited Juneau, Ketchikan, and Sagwa in Alaska and Victoria, in British Columbia. We saw Glacier Bay National Park, hiked the Chilkoot Trail, and did a zipline at Ketchikan. But as *time goes by* (hear the music from the movie *Casablanca* in the background), it was the people we met on the trip that I remember most.

I grin as I recall a Filipino woman from the cruise ship's cafeteria who sprayed our hands with disinfectant while saying, "washie, washie, washie," as she was smiling all the time. Then there was our ship's (the Norwegian Pearl) captain. He dazzled us at the crew introduction show by pulling up his pants to display his socks, a red one on his left foot and a green one on the other. He said that is how he could figure out the nautical light rules—port (red) from starboard (green). Then, I think of Patricia, the eighty-something year old mother of a New Hampshire friend, who met us at the boat and gave us a tour of Ketchikan.

Hello again. I'm back for my Alaska reveille. I have been thinking a lot about life and what makes people tick. Watch it! Sorry. Quirky pun. I hold up my left arm and point to my wristwatch. It seems to me that one of the most basic characteristics of humans and perhaps other species is their drive to explore. Just look at each of our lives. From the moment of birth, we want to move. First, there is crawling and then walking. We want to explore our world and universe.

The history of history represents explorations of the earliest people. They ventured out of Africa. Where there was water, they built ships. If they lived along a river, they wanted to follow its course downstream and go the opposite direction to discover its source. Note the clever rhyme in the last sentence—cute. The popular television and movie series, *Star Trek*, was based on the classic line "To Boldly Go Where No Man Has Gone Before…" The history of Europe in the 1600s featured explorations of routes to the Far East. When Thomas Jefferson orchestrated the Louisiana Purchase, he immediately dispatched Lewis and Clark to see the region. NASA is focused on exploring the universe. First, we went to the moon, and now, we want to go to Mars. We are explorers.

Yet people also say "there is no place like home." People enjoy the familiar. They often go to the same supermarket each time although there are several to pick from. We become creatures of habit. We take the same route to work each day. Most families eat a series of similar meals each week: spaghetti on Monday, veggie burgers on Tuesday, etc. So we want to explore, and we want to stay home. Perhaps, another way to put it is we want to have our cake and eat it, too. There remains the classic sailor's predicament. When a sailor is on shore, he longs to be on the sea; when at sea, he longs to be at the port. So to tie it all together, we want to explore and have adventures, yet at that same time, we appreciate being at home. This is yet another form of ambivalence.

A kissing cousin to ambivalence ranks the notion of simultaneous opposites. Here we cling to two simultaneously contradictory ideas. The statement, you want to both fit in and stand out at the same time captures the dilemma. Watch a group of people. It could be at school, work, or a social gathering. On one hand, you want to be accepted. Yes, people want to be part of a gang or a club. Yet on the other hand, you like to see you are perceived as an individual. You are unique. And in the words of the Frank Sinatra lyrics, "I did it my way." Or as Garrison Keillor says in *Lake Wobegon Days*, everybody is unique, just like everyone else.

Another example of these simultaneous opposites occurs when one goes to the doctor. You present the physician with a number of symptoms. You do not know what they all mean, but you know you are sick. After the doctor takes history and conducts a physical examination, the practitioner determines a diagnosis and sets out a treatment plan. You are immediately relieved that your symptoms fit a pattern that has been seen before. Yet you feel a bit let down that you are neither unique nor unusual. You fit a pattern and have gotten a standard prescription. You are relieved and disappointed at the same time.

In the spirit of simultaneous opposites, I will make one further point. We, as human beings, are hardwired to hold contrasting views. We are complex and confounding persons. Here is what I mean. We hold within ourselves contradictory ideas and beliefs and practice totally inconsistent behaviours. For example, in *The Godfather Series,* many of the main characters are portrayed as very pious, worshiping people who regularly violate the Ten Commandments. And that also what makes each of us such amazing and fascinating unique individuals.

The Unions of Opposites by Bruce Hathaway

Conclusion

Finally, what is the take-home message on ambivalence? It is simple. Every decision you will make and every relationship you will have, contains ambivalence. You will both love and resent your mate at the same time. School and work will be both fun and a pain. Enjoy the ride.

References

Frost, R. Mending Walls begins with "Something there is that doesn't love a wall, ...and ends with "Good fences make good neighbors." http://writing.upenn.edu/~afilreis/88/frost-mending.html accessed 3/23/18.

Scott, J. Treasured Volume: An Anthology of Poems, 1967. New York, N.Y., The Oak Tree Press, Inc.

CHAPTER 3

The Heart Versus the Head

Follow your bliss.

—Joseph Campbell

Decide on what you think is right, and stick to it.
—George Eliot

Better to be without logic than without feeling.
—Charlotte Bronte

Hello, all, it is time to look at life through the lens of one's body. By now, in reading this book, you might start to roll your eyes up. And you silently mutter, "There he goes again." (This is a paraphrasing of a quote from the presidential debate on October 28, 1980, where Ronald Reagan said to President Jimmy Carter, "There you go again.") If you had guessed, I am being needlessly obtuse and provocative. You were right.

I selected a corporal introduction to entice you into the next topic. It is the classic dilemma of whether to follow the tenets of your heart or to pursue what is logical and reasonable, biologically speaking, the battle between your gut feelings and your brain; hence, the reference to one's own body. An alternative framework would be right brain versus left brain.

My Snood computer game

Heart versus head is playing right now for me. I am debating whether to write this chapter or to play a computer game called Snood. So here is the conflict. Logic says I should be writing. But my heart says you've got to play it until you reach a certain score. Well, in the genuine spirit of this chapter, the game won out. I did reach the level I wanted, and now, I can continue writing this chapter. This debate reflects also on my ambivalence about writing.

However, in typical fashion, I want to go two ways simultaneously. I wish to discuss the word *should*, and I want to talk about the heart versus the head. Let us look at should first.

The operative word is *should*, and life is dominated by shoulds. People bombard all of us with an endless cavalcade of what you should—what you should say, what you should wear, and how you should feel. Commonly, people will inform you of the proper emotion for an experience. They have no regard nor do they listen to how you really feel. A friend responded to a complaining woman with the following pronouncement, "You have two legs and two arms, so you should feel good." He had completely discounted her emotions and totally focused on his own criteria as the basis of for *her* feelings.

Now, to be honest, there are a number of important shoulds that really do matter. Perhaps there are the Ten Commandments. In the Judeo-Christian world, these form the cornerstone of rules of the road. And speaking of roads, speed limits visibly proclaim the speed you should drive at. So I am not about to dismiss all the shoulds. What I am saying is that you will encounter the shoulds that are not only others wish to impose upon you but also find those which you demand of yourself. The example is what you might say to yourself you "should get the grade of 'A'" in a class. In other words, you tell yourself you should receive an A in that course. And this interior requirement can become an immensely powerful motivator or a source of guilt.

Now back to the theme of this chapter. When people suggest what you should do, they are telling what is logical for you to do based on their value system. But here comes the rub. Often, what you should do contradicts what *you* want to do. What *you* want to do represents a synonym of what your heart is telling you and your gut feeling.

Let me tell you another story. Monday was July 5, which is the day after the actual July 4, our Independence Day holiday. We had some guests over to enjoy the lake, swim, eat, and be merry. However, in the middle of the afternoon, I had to take your Aunt Matana back to her mother's home in Haverhill, Massachusetts. So we motored down the highway. I dropped her off and almost headed back. But and life and these situations are full of buts, the New Balance sneaker company has its factory outlet in Lawrence. That is a neighboring town to Haverhill. Logically, I had guests and family to be responsible for. That means returning swiftly and directly. But yes, back to the but, I really, really, really wanted a new pair of jogging shoes. I love jogging. So I did what I wanted. I went to the outlet and came home later than I should have.

Oh my god, I have missed the elephant in the room. It is love. Love represents the ultimate triumph of the heart over logic. Indeed, the heart is the symbol of love in Valentine's Day. Or as Dante pens in his *Divine Comedy*, "The love that moves the sun and the other stars." Westley and Foster, love propelled your mother and your father to marry. It is the reason Peggy and I are together.

Love serves as the basis of the so-called "Hollywood ending." Here, in the movie's dilemma, people who society, their families, and friends say should not be together ultimately follow their hearts and marry. In the typical scenario, two people from different religions, races, ethnic groups, educational experiences, political parties, socioeconomic groups, or sides of the tracks overcome those hurdles and get married. They then ride off into the sunset and live happily ever after. Spoiler alert, the subject of love will be revisited in the book's last chapter.

Then, of course, there is the old chestnut. How many psychiatrists does it take to change a light bulb? The answer is one, provided the bulb really wants to change! So people often do what they really want to do rather than what they should do.

Yet my only example right now is I am having to choose between working more or playing golf. My head says, "You have papers to write, things to accomplish, and student assignments to check." My heart quietly announces, "You love golf even though you are not good at it." So I am off to play golf.

Conclusion

So what's the answer? Pay attention to what is logical, but go with your heart and gut feelings.

References

Bronte, C. "Better…without feeling." https://www.goodreads.com/quotes/23764-better-to-be-without-logic-than-without-feeling accessed 3/23/18.

Campell, J. "Follow your bliss", https://www.goodreads.com/quotes/tag/follow-your-bliss, accessed 3/23/18.

Eilot, G. "Decide on…stick to it.", https://www.quotes.net/quote/43622 accessed 3/23/18.

Reagan, R. https://www.youtube.com/watch?v=Wi9y5-Vo61w accessed 9/18/18.

CHAPTER 4

Alone or as Part of a Group

To be alone or a part of the group? That is the question Thank you, William Shakespeare. This fourth chapter looks at the decision to do things solo or as part of a group.

Quotes
Alone

> I think this is the most extraordinary collection of talent, of human knowledge that has ever been gathered together at the White House, with the possible exception of when Thomas Jefferson dined alone. Someone once said that Thomas Jefferson was a gentleman of thirty-two who could calculate an eclipse, survey an estate, tie an artery, plan an edifice, try a cause, break a horse, and dance the minuet. (John F. Kennedy, An Extract from His Remarks at a Dinner Honoring Nobel Prize Winners of the Western Hemisphere in April 29, 1962)

> None of us will ever accomplish anything excellent or commanding except when he listens

to this, whisper which is heard by him alone. ((Ralph Waldo Emerson)

I love to be alone. I never found a companion that was so companionable as solitude. (Henry David Thoreau)

Do not wait for leaders; do it alone, person to person. (Mother Teresa of Calcutta)

Be yourself. Above all, let who you are, what you are, what you believe shine through every sentence you write, every piece you finish. (John Jakes)

The four cornerstones of character, on which the structure of this nation was built, are Initiative, Imagination, Individuality, and Independence. (Edward Vernon Rickenbacker)

As Part of a Group

Never doubt that a small group of thoughtful, committed citizens can change the world; indeed, it's the only thing that ever has. (Margaret Mead)

Coming together is a beginning. Keeping together is progress. Working together is success. (Henry Ford)

Individual commitment to a group effort— that is what makes a team work, a company work, a society work, a civilization work. (Vince Lombardi)

You will notice that this chapter begins with an extraordinary series of quotations. The idea of doing things alone, by yourself, or as part of a group emerges as complicated, passionately argued, and dependent on the situation. In other words, this one is not easy. Let me start with an example of how complex this duality can be.

In sports, there are individual and team sports. Simple? Not really. Golf is an individual sport. Agreed. It really does reflect on the person's skills, talents, and determination. So one player does win the tournament, or in the case of The Masters, one individual goes home in the coveted green jacket. Yet even in golf, there can be teams. On the international level, there is the Ryder Cup, which pits American versus European teams against each other. This biennial tournament began in 1927. Or, in the more local approach, I have played on teams in what is called "best ball." In this case, you are on a team with three other players. In this format, one team plays against other teams. It begins with all four members of the team teeing off. Then they select which of the drives was the best. Next, all four again hit from the location of the best ball, and so on. Thus, the team has one score for each hole. The point here, is that even in the highly individualized game of golf, it can be team-based too.

Or let's go to the other part of the spectrum with the classic team sport, baseball. Yes, if you win, it's because the team wins. Yet individual performance also applies. If the pitcher throws a no hitter, it usually means you win. But in order to achieve that no-hitter distinction, other players have to do outstanding defense, great catches, and throwing outs, as well timing hitting on the offense side. Again, individual statistics testify to the importance of a person's performance—RBI (runs batted in), batting average, and number of errors committed. Yet it is the team that wins the World Series.

But that is sports. What about in work? I write alone. Word crafting is very solitary. May I also add that, in writing, ambivalence plays a major part. I love to write, but I also hate to write. I cannot tell how many times I will interrupt my typing to play Snood, a computer game, or to do other rituals I employ to avoid writing. So the bottom line is that writing is done alone. Yet I also rely on others to edit my work. Thank you, my editors.

In healthcare, team work is essential. The team of doctors, nurses, nutritionists, occupational therapists, housekeepers, and administrative personnel all play a role. Yet the role of physicians cannot be overstated. Again, in the operating room, the surgeon remains key, but that person is supported by an anesthesiologist, surgical nurses, other doctors, and technicians. Recently, I had a bout with prostate cancer. For forty-four days—nine weeks of daily treatment on weekdays; not on weekends—a huge expensive radiation machine zapped me for about five minutes from seven angles. Sure, my physician set the course, so to speak, but it was the crew that made it work. There were nurses, social workers, dietitians, receptionists, office managers, and technicians who were dedicated to make the treatment successful. It was a team effort.

It is often said that statues are not erected to teams but rather to individuals. In any trip about any metropolitan area or battlefield, you will see proudly displayed statues honoring individuals—politicians and generals. But let me take you to a time when the team should have had a statue erected to it. Apollo 13 ranks as one of the greatest team efforts. It began with "Houston, we have a problem." A capsule malfunction imperiled not only the lunar landing mission but also the lives of the entire crew of three. As the capsule headed to its premature return to earth, the cabin's carbon dioxide reached dangerous levels. Back at mission control, the commander hastily convened a group of workers in a room. They only had items available in the actual Apollo 13 capsule to use. Their marching order was "failure is not an option." Together, they swiftly crafted a device which would remove the carbon dioxide inside the spaceship and save the crew's lives. Team effort here was at its best. And the crew returned to home earth alive!

Let me take a different tact. In certain situations, a group is required. In Judaism, there is the concept of a *minyan*. This has been called the quorum for prayer. In the strictest sense, the Orthodox Jews need originally ten men, all of whom have had a bar mitzvah, in order to say certain prayers in a synagogue. Later, women were allowed to count in the Conservative and Reform movements. But the bottom line is you have to have ten people for a minyan. The group becomes paramount. So for example, in the practice of *yahrzeit*, which is saying *kaddish*, a memorial prayer on the anniversary of the death of a loved one, most often a parent, you need ten people in the synagogue. In any case, here is an example of the need and power of the group, where you cannot do it alone. And there are other situations requiring a group too, such as a trial jury.

Time to go in a new direction, jogging. I love to jog. As I jog, I think. I have discovered, when my foot hits the pavement, that I move into a remarkably productive contemplation mode. I reflect on the world, come up with new ideas, or solve problems. I recall one day I was out, jogging and feeling rather down, because a book I was writing under contract was cancelled by the publisher. My many hours of work seemed wasted. As the miles passed below my feet, an idea came to me. I could convert the concept of the book about managed care into a series of articles written by my more knowledgeable colleagues on that subject into a journal issue. I could edit that journal. So I called a journal's publisher. She liked the idea. So, the idea, which came to me while jogging and thinking, set-up the solution to my problem.

I have composed much of this book while jogging. Sometimes, I think of things I want to say. Other times, I will start out with an idea but not how to phrase it. The jog allows me an opportunity to rehearse several versions. But when I do get home and am at the computer, I will yet again change it.

Let me take jogging on a different route. The actual jog itself need not be a solitary activity. I often used to jog with a running buddy. One of my favorite hoof companions was another psychiatrist, John Iwuc. Running with a partner allowed us to run farther. And chatting en route was a great stress reliever for both of us. We bounced ideas and problems off each other. One memorable run, we were talking about relationships. He noted the success of his marriage was how he resolved arguments with his wife. He would ultimately have to decide if that disagreement was worth the relationship. He always concluded that the marriage was more important than the area under contention. So two minds can be better than one in jogging too! Others, by the way, will run in groups, with benefits for all of them.

Halloween 2017; Catman, a.k.a. Foster, and
Alexander Hamilton, a.k.a. Westley.

New direction. Thus far, I have focused on ideas and contradictions. It is time to turn the tables. Here is an example how others have taught me. I remember a team meeting I used to lead. I would begin with an agenda. But the group's success came when they offered their opinions and wandered off the topic, too. They had brilliant insights and furnished innovative ways of approaching a problem. They suggested methods which I had never dreamed of. And Westley and Foster contributed to this book in many ways. Here is one example how. Yes, your mother crafted these amazing Halloween costumes, but it was your energy and essence which gave them personality and power. The team meant your mother and her starring two sons.

My partner, Peggy Tucker, gave me new insights into the doing things alone versus with others. She was contemplating on going to the Deerfield Fair. This is an annual event in the late September, featuring agricultural activities and neat community events. She has gone for many years either alone or often with a friend or her daughter or myself. For her, it is a great experience, especially the horse-pulling contest where teams of horses compete to which can pull the heaviest load. So this year, she wonders whether to go alone or with someone. The pros of going alone include seeing things and activities at her own pace. The reason to go with another person is to be able to share the experience with someone. I, too, am curious as to which she will choose. PS, it was Peggy who came up with the title for this book.

Well, my grandchildren, in the words and song title by Bob Dylan, "*The Times, They Are A-Changin'*." Since I began this letter, which has taken some time, there has been a major change in your lives. So Westley, you now have a younger brother, Foster. So tangibly, that means the discussion of solo versus a group it is no longer just theoretical and academic. Now, solo, your only-child world has become a dyad. It is now Westley and Foster. So what does that mean? It no longer makes you the sole center of the family's attention. Yes, whether you want or care to, sharing will be a major factor in your life. But that is the immediate effect. But are a number of long-term gains. For example, it means having someone to share the family chores with.

Conclusions

In the end, you will have decided for yourselves. Sometimes you'll want to be alone and read. Other times, you'll wish to hike with a friend. Some days, you'll desire to do a solitary activity such as a game of solitaire or to play golf alone, some days, you'll like to play a team sport, such as in soccer or lacrosse. At a certain point, you plan to be leader; at another, you will follow. Life offers not only great opportunities, but also, it means picking between solo adventures and group activities. Choose wisely.

References

Donne, J. http://izquotes.com/quote/282566, 3/25/18.

Emerson, RW, https://www.goodreads.com/quotes/33230-none-of-us-will-ever-accomplish-anything-excellent-or-commanding 3/24/18.

Ford, H, https://www.goodreads.com/quotes/118854-coming-together-is-the-beginning-keeping-together-is-progress-working 3/25/18.

Jakes, J, https://www.brainyquote.com/quotes/john_jakes_201937 3/25/18.

Lombardi, V. http://www.vincelombardi.com/quotes.html, 3/25/18.

Kennedy, JF, http://tjrs.monticello.org/letter/1856 3/24/18.

Luccock, HE, https://www.slideshare.net/weekdone/15-powerful-team-building-quotes-to-inspire-successful-teamwork/12-No_one_can_whistlea_symphony, 3/25/18.

Mead, M, http://thinkexist.com/quotation/never_doubt_that_a_small_group_of_thoughtful/214732.html 3/25/18.

Mother Teresa of Calcutta, http://thinkexist.com/quotes/like/do_not_wait_for_leaders-do_it_alone-person_to/214997/, 3/25/18.

Rickenbacker, EV, http://www.azquotes.com/quote/245035 3/25/18.

Riley, P, http://thinkexist.com/quotation/great_teamwork_is_the_only_way_we_create_the/147091.html, 3/25/18.

Ruth, B, http://www.searchquotes.com/search/Team_Togetherness, 3/25/18.

Satoro, R, http://thinkexist.com/quotation/individually-we-are-one-drop-together-we-are-an/391196.html, 3/25/18.

Thoreau, HD, https://www.goodreads.com/quotes/17900-i-find-it-wholesome-to-be-alone-the-greater-part, 3/25/18.

CHAPTER 5

Rules Rule, or Do They?

Computers are like Old-Testament gods; lots of rules and no mercy.

—Joseph Campbell

A foolish consistency is the hobgoblin of little minds, adored by little statesmen and philosophers and divines.

—Ralph Waldo Emerson

Welcome back to yet another one of my six dueling dual messages of life. This one revolves around the question, when are rules important to follow, and when is it actually critical to break them? Westley and Foster and anyone who dares to recall their childhood, all your lives, you have been told or given rules to follow: when to go the sleep, when to get up, when to go to school, when to play, what to wear, and how to behave. And I know, firsthand, sometimes you adhere to these "suggestions," and sometimes you do your own thing.

In the adult world, rules rule. Rules carry with them consequences. When there is a job requirement that you must report to work on time and you are late, you could be fired. There are rules and laws to be obeyed. If not, there are real consequences. Yet it is not all that simple. In some circumstances, breaking a rule is the better course of action. To cut to the chase, in some instances, following the rules is the best, and on other occasions, it is better to challenge those dictates and break the rule.

Yet, as we will discover, obedience can be a complex subject. The best way to make this point is to illustrate it with two examples from World War II.

The First: Zigzag Rule

Zigzag Rule versus Steering a Straight Course

The story of the USS *Indianapolis* and the Japanese submarine illustrates how following rules or not, presents many complexities and dilemmas. (USS *Indianapolis* 2018 a, b) This is the story. At 12:14 a.m., on July 30, 1945, the USS *Indianapolis*, a heavy cruiser, was torpedoed by a Japanese submarine while traveling alone and unescorted in the Philippine Sea on course to Leyte. She sank in twelve minutes. Of 1,196 men on board, approximately three hundred went down with the ship. The remainder, about nine hundred men, were left floating in shark-infested waters, with no lifeboats and most with no food or water. The ship was never missed by the US Navy, and by the time the survivors were spotted by accident four days later, only 316 men were still alive.

The ship's captain, the late Charles Butler McVay III, survived and was court-martialed and convicted of "hazarding his ship by failing to zigzag." The Navy's zigzag rule was that vessels traveling in enemy waters must follow a zigzag route. This was instituted to make the ship more difficult to be torpedoed. The ironic part of this tale is that the US Navy would have never known fully what happened to the ship had it not been for the report by the Japanese submarine commander. When he surrendered at the end of the war, he noted initially that the ship was not zigzagging, and that is why his submarine had such a good shot at her.

So Captain McVay violated the zigzag rule. But that story is more complicated. Later testimony from the Japanese submarine commander revealed that zigzagging would have made no difference. Moreover, although over 350 navy ships were lost in combat in WWII, McVay was the only captain to be court-martialed. Over time, declassified material provided evidence that Captain McVay had been scapegoated for others' mistakes. The Navy had not informed Captain McVay that his cruiser was traveling in Japanese submarine-infested waters. Furthermore, the Navy failed to notice that the ship had not reached its port. As a result, on July 2001, the Navy department exonerated Captain McVay for the loss of USS *Indianapolis*. One further historical note, the USS *Indianapolis*'s mission before this tragedy was to deliver atomic bomb components to Tinian.

The Second: D-Day

June 6, 1944, Omaha Beach

On June 6, 1944, the long-awaited invasion of Normandy began, called D-Day. American troops stormed ashore on Omaha Beach. But the assault did not go as planned. Troops were trapped on the beach. The Army's forward artillery spotters could communicate with the battleships and cruisers to get their big-gun support. However, the guns did not fire because they feared not only hitting the German positions but also killing the GIs on the beaches. The Germans held the high ground and were slaughtering the Americans below. The destroyers had been ordered to withdraw from their offshore positions (Meyer 2018).

The destroyers' crews watched, with mounting horror, at the carnage. Finally, Lieut. Commander Ralph Ramey, the skipper of USS *McCook*, defied orders and aimed his ship forward and commenced firing at the enemy sites above the beach. Its cannons struck the German positions. The German firepower started to diminish. Soon, all the other destroyers joined in the attack and barrage, including USS *Frankford*. Its gunnery officer, Lieut. Owen Keeler, wrote, "A tank sitting at the water's edge, with a broken track, fired at something on the hill. We immediately followed up with a five-inch salvo. The tank gunner flipped open his hatch, looked around at us, waved, dropped back in the tank, and fired at another target. For the next few minutes, he was our fire-control party" (King, R. 2018).

Breaking the rules saved the day. The US Army thanked the US Navy (Knauer, 2004).

A White Mountains Example

During the fall of 1825, Samuel Willey Jr., along with his wife, five children, and two hired men, moved into a house in the heart of Crawford Notch in New Hampshire's White Mountains. That home would serve as an inn to accommodate travelers through the mountains on that desolate notch road. The first year, the three men enlarged and improved the house. The little cluster of buildings were situated in the shadow of what is now called Mount Willey. The following spring, there had been a prolonged drought period that had dried the mountain soil to an unusual depth.

Then, in the summer of 1826, there had been a series of rainstorms, followed by mudslides. These slides had been of such concern that the family developed an evacuation route and created a nearby shelter just in case their house was threatened. During the night of August 28, 1826, one of the most violent and destructive rainstorms ever known in the

White Mountains occurred. Mr. and Mrs. Willey, two children, and both hired men fled the house to take refuge in the emergency shelter.

Then something unexpected happened. There was a large boulder in front of the Willey home. "Down came the whole side of the mountain, in a cataract of ruin. Just before it reached the house, the stream broke into two branches—shivered not a window there but overwhelmed the whole vicinity, blocked up the road, and annihilated everything in its dreadful course" (Hawthorne). The quote from Hawthorne's short story "The Ambitious Guest", which based on the real Willey disaster story. Although the house was spared, all the inhabitants perished. The event gained national notoriety. As a result, people started coming to see the site, ushering in tourism to the White Mountains.

By now, you are wondering the reason for this story. It painfully illustrates how following the rules does not always work. The family and workers acted as planned. They followed their own rules. They were not saved.

Lessons from NASA

As noted in the introduction, at the Worcester Polytechnic Institute (W.P.I.) graduation in 2003, Ellen Ochoa gave the commencement address. She was the first Latino woman astronaut. In her talk, she described both how following NASA rules saved lives and how breaking them saved lives. Her talk showed decisions based on rules and one's adherence to them can lead to very different outcomes.

A Different Reason to Break the Rules

A cute old television advertisement for 100% Kosher Hebrew National Hot Dogs said, "They answer to a higher authority." Certainly, in jest, they were referring to a divine possible contribution to its product. So let us look at several examples where individuals selected to break the rules because of higher principles.

In July of 1846, the local sheriff arrested Henry David Thoreau and placed him in jail. He broke the law by not paying his poll tax. He knew that he had to pay it but had refused to do so since 1842. He reasoned that the poll tax helped finance the coming war with Mexico. He further believed that the war would lead to an expansion of the slavery in the United States. Ultimately, he wrote the book *Civil Disobedience.* In it and at the time, he argued one must not obey a government policy which was against one's conscience and principles.

Many others deliberately chose to not follow laws they did not feel were right. One was Mahatma Gandhi. He said, "It is contrary to our manhood if we obey laws repugnant to our conscience." Britain ruled India. England controlled all the salt production and its distribution. On March 12, 1930, Gandhi led a march from Sabarmati to the coastal town of Dandi on the Arabian Sea some 241 miles away. This was in defiance of the British authority and laws. Martin Luther King Jr.'s arrest and confinement offers yet another example of breaking rules for a higher purpose. As he wrote in his famous Letter from Birmingham Jail, "We will reach the goal of freedom in Birmingham and all over the nation, because the goal of America is freedom."

See how complicated things can become with rules? Normally, you would think of people who deliberately broke the law and are arrested as criminals. Psychiatry classifies these folks as antisocial personalities. People who have an antisocial personality have no regard for the rules of society and show no compassion when hurting others. Yet Thoreau, Gandhi, and King consciously broke the social rules to improve society.

Rules not Enforced

If the rule dilemma were not complex enough, here is another wrinkle. Society has some rules which, they say, maybe okay to break. Confusing? Let me give you some examples. In many of the colleges and universities in which I have taught, the administration posts the following notice, "No eating and drinking allowed in this classroom." What actually happens is both students and faculty eat and enjoy beverages during the class. The officials do not enforce that rule. Or, as you will see, people will be driving on an Interstate highway at seventy miles per hour (MPH) when the posted speed limit is six-ty-five MPH. Basically and informally, the police say they will only ticket you if you are exceeding the speed limit, by ten MPH over the limit. These are all examples of when and where authorities actually disregard a law and simply do not enforce it. Yes, that is confusing.

Conclusion

As you have realized by now, choosing whether to follow rules or not is not simple. Generally, if there is a sign saying "Don't walk," you should wait. Then when the sign says, "Walk," you can then walk. Similarly, when driving, stop for a red light. But as these exam-ples illustrated, in some situations, one might run the light after looking both ways, if one had to get an injured person to a hospital.

References

Campbell, J, http://thinkexist.com/quotation/computers_are_like_ old_testament_gods-lots_of/152696.html 3/27/18.

Editors of Time, D-DAY: 24 Hours That Saved the World, May 24, 2004, New York, Time, p 55-56.

Emerson, RW, http://quotesnack.com/ralph-waldo-emerson/a-fool-ish-consistency-is-the-hobgoblin-of-little-minds-ralph-waldo-emerson 3/27/1.

Gandi, M, http://www.kamat.com/mmgandhi/civil_disobedience. htm. 3/31/18.

Gandhi leads civil disobedience, https://www.history.com/this-day-in-history/gandhi-leads-civil-disobedience. 3/31/18.

Hawthorne, N, "The Ambitious Guest" http://www.eastoftheweb.com/short-stories/UBooks/AmbGue.shtml 3/28/18.

King, ML, https://www.theatlantic.com/politics/archive/1963/08/martin-luther-kings-letter-from-birmingham-jail/274668 3/31/18.

King, R. Dr. Yale Kamer. http://www.ruthfullyyours.com/2014/06/06/dr-yale-kramer-the-navys-heroic-role-in-normandy/ 11/21/18.

Knauer, Time: D-Day: 24 Hours That Saved the World Hardcover—May 24, 2004, New York, Time Magazine.

Meyer, R E and Rutte, T, D-Day Invasion http://articles.latimes.com/1994-05-31/news/wr-64225_1_d-day-invasion/12 11/21/18.

Navy. (Time, Editors, 2004 Wow, here breaking rules not only saved lives but also made history.

Ochoa, E, https://www.encyclopedia.com/people/history/historians-miscellaneous-biographies/ellen-ochoa 3/28/18.

Sears, JF, "The Ambitious Guest" and the Significance of the Willey Disaster, *American Literature*, Vol. 54, No. 3 (Oct., 1982), pp. 354-367.

Thoreau, HD, http://historyofmassachusetts.org/henry-david-thoreau-arrested-for-nonpayment-of-poll-tax 3/29/18.

Share *Facebook Twitter Pinterest.*

USS Indianapolis a, http://www.ussindianapolis.org/ 11/19/2018.

USS Indianapolis-b https://www.history.navy.mil/browse-by-topic/disasters-and-phenomena/indianapolis.html 11/20/18.

CHAPTER 6

The Big Picture, Forward Movement, and Everyday Life

Rainbow over Crawford Notch, White
Mountains, New Hampshire

A satisfied customer is the best business strategy
of all.

—Michael LeBoeuf

Strategy without tactics is the slowest route
to victory. Tactics without strategy is the noise
before defeat.

—Sun Tzu

Hello. Already to embark on a new idea? It is the concept and appreciation of having a major goal in your life. That objective can frame the big picture for your life. Having such a vision has several benefits. It allows you to take the immediate steps to achieve that mission. It suggests things to do when the goal cannot be gained immediately. And it gives you perspective and perseverance.

This is sounding a bit obtuse and looks a little murky. In fact, there are two ways in which the big picture provides a life's framework. In the first instance, you are proceeding toward a goal. And you take specific steps immediately to reach it. In the second, you have a big-picture idea, but it is not achievable at that moment. So you do other things until the time is right. Let me offer examples of each.

Having a Goal with Immediate Steps to Achieve It

I climb mountains in New Hampshire, Maine, and Vermont. The big picture for me is planning a route, a.k.a. selecting a trail to follow. My goal remains fixed—to climb that mountain. Yes, if I were more talented and dramatic, I would have us all break into the song "Climb Every Mountain" from *The Sound of Music* by Rodgers and Hammerstein.

> Climb every mountain,
> Search high and low,
> Follow every byway,
> Every path you know…
> Climb every mountain,
> Ford every stream,
> Follow every rainbow
> Till you find your dream.

But alas, I have yet again digressed. My point is, the goal or the big picture is to climb the mountain and reach the summit. You pick a trail to follow. But that is just part of the journey. There is a very effective advertisement for a stock market brokerage, called Dean

Witter, which says, "We measure success one investor at a time." Now what does that have to do with mountain climbing? Simply this. You hike up and down the mountain, one step at a time. Yes, you are marching toward a goal. Yet one false step and you'll lose your footing. With the results, you twist your ankle, or you could even fall off the mountain. So you pay attention to each step.

Let me venture another example. I used to have a Pearson thirty-six-foot sailboat, which was moored at the Portland Yacht Club. Sounds very neat. And it was. Westley and Foster's grandfather, a.k.a. me, and at certain times, your father, were in the sail set. Every August, we took part in a famous sailboat race called the Monhegan. The first race was held in 1928. The race begins in Casco Bay. Sailboats go around Monhegan Island in Penobscot Bay and return near the starting point. It is an overnight race, covering approximately 120 miles. There is a shorter version called the Manana, which rounds Manana Island and covers about 90 miles. This one was for smaller sailboats, such as mine. So before we started the race, I would go down into the cabin and rolled out the nautical chart to see the big picture. I looked at all the navigation markers we needed to reach and round for the entire race. The course to each "mark" represented a leg. And the Manana had many legs. Each mark had to be achieved in the proper order and rounded correctly to complete the race.

How Road Maps Differ from Nautical Charts

Warning, a major digression coming! What's the difference between a map and a chart? Good question, and glad you asked it. Maps are often most typified as road maps. These maps show you the various highways and places along the route. Charts are used in water travel, and they show shoreline, water depths, and hazards. Okay, what's the big deal? Or as in the old advertisement for Wendy's, "Where's the beef?"

Maps show you where you can only go. Hence, it outlines the roads you can drive on. Unless you drive a tank or a neat jeep, you are confined to roads. Maps are like straitjackets; they tell only where you can go in a car. On the other hand, charts tell you only where you *cannot* go. If the shoreline is too rocky or the depth is not enough, you must avoid those areas. Yet excluding those places, what a chart provides a graphic to show you everywhere you can go! The possibilities on charts are endless.

So returning to the Manana race, I plotted out the entire race first on a chart. Then, in the actual race, we sailed each leg.

Oh my god, yet another interruption. I like to tell jokes. And I think they are funny. However, not everyone agrees with me. My son, Barak, Westley and Foster's uncle, once said that because of my jokes, I was in danger of being "voted off the table" (a classic line from the TV show *Survivor*). So in the race, as we approached each mark, such as a buoy or a nun, the team was excited. It was important not to hit it or miss rounding it. Failure to round it properly meant we would be forced to repeat the maneuver, losing valuable time. Hence, the approach to mark came high stress anxiety. My way to deal with it was to tell jokes. The fear of hearing my humor galvanized the crew into action. The quicker the mark was gained correctly, the fewer the jokes. Remember, the big picture goal was to finish and perhaps to win the race, but that could only be done one leg at a time.

The Other Situation, When the Goal Cannot Be Gained Immediately

Let me jump to a concrete example. I love to write, so one of my life's goals is to spend time writing. Yes, I wish to write the greatest American novel or at least a decent book. I know I have authored a number of books, but I still keep striving. So in one sense, I live to write, and this book stands for one of my life's accomplishments. I digress for a very brief moment. I both love and hate to write simultaneously. I covered that topic in chapter two, Ambivalence.

Returning to the main point. Writing has been my passion and beacon. It has been my guide and the clarion call. It is my motivation and my North Star. But it does not pay the rent. Now I teach, which I also enjoy. But life forced me to not write all the time. Let me go back to the days when I was an emergency psychiatrist in the emergency department at a large teaching hospital. I would see and help many patients during the day. I loved that job. But what sustained me was to write a book about psychiatric emergencies, which I worked on after your aunt, Sasha, and your father, Ben went to bed. My real passion and goal was writing; my income depended on seeing patients.

A Jogging Example of Doing Two Things at the Same Time

Major digression alert. I will be talking about the idea of doing more than one activity at the same time. For me, jogging is my significant exercise activity as well as method to manage stress and control my weight. And now to return to the two-things-at-one-time message.

If jogging alone is good, running with companion is even better. By doing so, we not only exercise but also have a great conversation at the same time—double benefits. I recall fondly jogging with a colleague when I worked at a state psychiatric hospital in Massachusetts. As we rounded a small lake on the hospital's campus, we shared ideas about work, life, dreams and aspirations. We jogged and gained insights. It was really a three for one event, we exercised, talked which helped us deal with our stresses and burned calories rather than ingesting them.

The trail to the summit

2019—the 200th Anniversary of the Crawford Path

Back to the Theme of the Big Picture, Forward Movement, and Everyday Life

Life is full of decisions—whether to live and work toward a goal yet, at the same time, recognize that you have to earn a living. That is the question. Thank you again, *Hamlet,* this time. There is an old joke (all my jokes are old because I am old). A neurotic person dreams of castles in the sky, a psychotic individual lives in castles in the sky, and the psychiatrist charges the rent. It is important to keep a dream, a goal, and a path while, at the same time, being grounded or doing things for every day survival.

The Big Picture Gives You Perspective

Having a big goal allows you to accept and tolerate many of life's challenges, disappointments, and defeats. The major objective can give you perspective. Here are two examples.

In the first one, someday, God-willing, and when the tuition has been paid, you, my grandsons, will go to college. There, you will ultimately select a major and aim toward a career. In school, you will encounter a special breed of students. These are the prelaw and premed school students. Their goal in attending college is to get into a law school or a medical school. They often differ from some of your other classmates in the way they study. These are the students who work very hard on the assignments and laboratories. Many will sadly but realistically focus on their grades. Some of them are very competitive. They know their goal—a law or medical school. They can tolerate and put up with a great deal of classwork. Their having a goal, directs them, in contrast, other students seem to wander about and waste time.

My model of the Charles W. Morgan

The other example is a little more off the course but provides a way of seeing the goal as a sustaining life force. For years I did emergency psychiatry and had a small private psychiatric practice. It was good. I helped many people, helped them to resolve numerous problems, and earned a reasonable living. But at the end of the day, what did I have to show for all my efforts? Certainly, they constituted "billable" events, a good accountant term. I have prevented some people from taking their own lives, called suicide. On some days, I've even stopped a homicide. I've helped people discover their inner child, happiness, and goal. I've facilitated them gaining ego strength. Some of my patients gained insight and experienced what is called an *aha* moment when they realize something about themselves and their relationship to others. And, of course, there was a pile of paperwork to document the day's activities.

But still, I wanted something more tangible that I could show what I had done for the day. I violated one of the Ten Commandments. I coveted what carpenters did. They could actually show, for all to see, the fruits of their labor, such as a chair or a cabinet. However, I was not a carpenter. But I did like to make models, especially model ships. So I bought an 890-piece wood model ship kit. It happens to be of the Charles W. Morgan, the last of the great whaling barks now permanently berthed at Mystic Seaport in Mystic, Connecticut.

It took me seven and a half years to finish building that model ship. Right now, it is displayed under a plexiglass case on my credenza. Each night, I did a little work on it. I sanded or painted the spars, masts, decks, and hull. I had a hull of a time. I put thread through the deadeyes and secured the masts. And each day, when I was done, I could not only show what I had accomplished, but it was also there for the next day to build on. Having the model ship to work on, provided me with a focus and a perspective to deal with daily challenges.

Having a Goal Gives You Perseverance

Once, when asked to give his definition of genius, Mr. Edison replied, "Two percent is genius and ninety-eight percent is hard work." (Thomas A. Edison)

Having a goal allows you to be persistent and to have perseverance. The famous race depicted in the fable "The Tortoise and the Hare" provides an excellent example. What I am extolling is the value of keeping on track, staying the course, and keeping on plugging away. So here, I will connect the big picture and the daily achievements. It is the idea of just keeping moving forward.

This winter 2015, in New England, we have record a snowfall and two blizzards. As a variation to the lyrics from *Oklahoma*, "The corn is as high as an elephant's eye," we had snow as high as an elephant's eye. Each time it snowed, we shoveled the walks, cleared the deck, made a path for the oil delivery, used the snow blower on the driveway, and raked the roof. It was repetitive, with storm after storm and shoveling after shoveling. Yet had we not kept that up, we eventually would be trapped in the house, and the roof might have collapsed. So we kept on moving forward; one foot in front of the other.

Returning to the Other Situation, When the Goal Cannot Be Gained Immediately

Well, life events often interfere with, disrupt and delay moving towards a goal. What to do when the goal is not immediately achievable right now? I am in one of those periods where the big picture eludes me and life goes on. I am about to head north, to the White Mountains of New Hampshire. Specifically, I will drive to Pinkham Notch. There, I will spend the next two days mentoring a newbie Information Volunteer for the Appalachian Mountain Club, a.k.a. AMC. It is not climbing and summiting a mountain, but it at least gets me to the mountains. And I am certainly not writing the great American novel at that moment.

A Chessboard Example for Your Life's Moves

And that reminds me of one of the greatest lessons in life taught to me by one of my Cheshire Academy teachers, Mr. Paul Boyd. Besides being an English professor, he served as the faculty advisor to the chess club. Mr. Boyd had a few basic rules for chess. I think there were eight. One of them went something like, "Castle as soon as possible." The one appropriate here was, "If you cannot make a good move, don't make a bad move." In this case, going to the mountains and working as a volunteer was *not* a bad move. Besides *not* being a bad move, the trip has many possibilities and many opportunities. I could think about the next chapter, I could network, and I could write articles for the AMC newsletter.

A digression to explore the concepts of convergence and divergence

Hello, it is time to develop a by-product of the concept of the big picture, convergence. This is where little pieces come together and make one conclusion. The easiest example of this convergence comes from a college course called Human Sexuality, which I taught. The subject matter relied on the contributions from the disciplines of biology, physiology, philosophy, psychology, and sociology. And this class offers a great example of convergence, the phenomena of menstrual synchrony. This is the amazing situation of, if a number of women who live in very close proximity to one another, such as in dormitory, within a short time, they will all be on the same menstrual cycle. This is called menstrual synchrony. Each woman's pheromones (chemical messengers), in conjunction with the olfactory (sense of smell) system and endocrine organs, bring this about. It nicely illustrates the convergence of specific information from several disciplines to explain a phenomenon.

Perhaps a better example of convergence happened to me this year. I have heard that one of the values of meditation is the ability to lose one's self-identity and instead to feel a sense of connectedness. That experience allows one to enter into an almost out-of-body event. Last month, I started the *Great Courses* series on the Neurobiology of Religion. As an aside, I listen to or watch educational CDs and DVDs, while I am on the elliptical exercise machine. Yet, another example of doing two things at the same time—exercising and learning. In the lectures, the physician talked about using radioactive chemicals, such as glucose, a.k.a. sugar, to show which parts of the brain are active. The activity is registered by the rate of glucose utilization.

People who were studied in deep meditation state, had less of this chemical being metabolized in the area of the brain's cerebral cortex, where the parietal and temporal lobes come together. Furthermore, it has been shown that the junction of the parietal and temporal lobes is responsible for one's sense of identity. The selflessness state, through meditation, has been confirmed by neurofunctional imaging. Yet another example of convergence.

Go figure. Once I got started on this convergence kick, I keep on finding more examples. So just the other day, I was again exercising on my elliptical exercise machine, and this time, I was learning via DVD about statistics. As another loose association, in college and medical school, we called statistics, *sadistic* because it was so hard to understand. But I digress. Yet another thought—two things govern my daily life, exercise and learning something new.

Meanwhile, in the statistics course, the lecturer talked about the formula for radioactive decay. The basic concept involves that randomly individual atoms actually change into another atom. The point here was that this statistical course helped me to understand the geologic phenomena of dating rocks using the half-life equation. In other words, it was convergence.

The opposite of convergence is divergence. Let us take a look at divergence thinking. It is also called nonconventional thinking. A quick way to understand the two is that convergence results in one answer; divergence leads to many solutions.

Here is a simple example of divergent thinking. Take the word "rat." What can that word mean? It is a rodent crawling in the basement or the alley. It was the carrier of the Bubonic Plague, also known as the black death. If you are a jogger on the island of Saint Thomas, you'll see signs asking you to become a RAT, which translates into Runners Against Trash. It urges you to pick up litter. If it were a gangster movie, a rat would be someone who informs on the gang, as to rat someone out. Gangsters make one think of other movies, and that leads to the Rat Pack, consisting of Frank Sinatra, Dean Martin, Sammy Davis Jr., Peter Lawford and Joey Bishop among others. Go the other way; there is the Rat Race. The capitalist competitive jungle one works in. Thus, this is how to define rat by divergent thinking.

So to circle back to the big picture, forward movement and everyday life theme. Either, start with a big picture issue or an everyday life situation. Each can be viewed through these two different lenses. Convergence gives you in one answer. Divergence offers an explosion of possibilities. Depending on the problem, one of the two routes will provide the solution.

The Difference between Strategy and Tactics: Another Way to See the Big Picture

Thus far, I having been talking about the big picture and the steps required to reach a goal—the summit and the yacht race finish marker. I will shift gears and talk about the difference between strategy and tactics to illustrate another dimension to the big picture. Strategy is the act of winning the war, and tactics are the methods of winning the battle. Wars are made up of battles. And yes, you can lose the battle and win the war, and vice versa, win the battle and lose the war.

Let me provide an example which is very dear my heart. I was born on December 7, 1942. That was a year to the day after the Japanese attack on Pearl Harbor, which resulted in the American declaration of war in World War II. Or as President Roosevelt said, "A day that shall live in infamy." This was a huge military defeat for the United States. Over three thousand sailors, soldiers, and other people were killed. and many warships were damaged or sunk, including the battleship Arizona. Yet it turns out seemingly that loss proved to be a strategic victory. How so? Good question. First, before that attack, there was a giant naval debate as to which were more important, battleships or aircraft carriers. Dramatically, that attack said, decisively, it were the aircraft carriers! As it developed, all the battleships that were sunk, except for the Arizona, were refloated and used by the end of the war. The Nevada provided naval support for the invasion of Normandy.

Furthermore, none of the repair facilities in Hawaii had been hit, so the base could return to operation relatively swiftly. None of the huge fuel depots had been hit. So the fuel stores was totally intact for other missions. And most importantly, none of the US aircraft carriers were in port at the moment of the attack. As a result, three US carriers, the Enterprise, Hornet, and Yorktown, launched planes against the four aircraft carriers of Japan as they were readying aircraft to attack the island of Midway. The American airplanes sunk all four Japanese carriers while the US did lose one, the Yorktown. The fact that US carriers had escaped the attack on Pearl Harbor set up the naval turning point in the Pacific off Midway. So Pearl Harbor represented a tactical loss but a strategic victory.

A Pause to Review

Hello, all. I am writing you from the Appalachian Mountain Club's (AMC) Highland Center, located in Crawford Notch, New Hampshire. It is early evening, and in the immediate distance, I hear the sound of thunder. Today was a "down day" for me. That means I was not scheduled to do any "work." So I am using it as an example of the big picture as a way to review some of its points.

The reason for this down day was that last night, I gave a talk at the Highland Center to a small but appreciative audience called "The Wilderness Speaks." It was about how the sunshine provides the energy for the earth, how rocks and trees tell time and how and why the birds sing, as well as the importance of water for life on earth. Tomorrow, I will work as an Information Volunteer. Hence, I found myself with unscheduled time. Sounds good, but I do not like that. I prefer to be active and productive. In fact, one of the mottos guiding my life was a statement that was on a synagogue calendar in my parent's kitchen. It said, "Oh, God, I have not wasted today."

So I used the free time by jogging, then doing our adoptive trail work, and finally, writing the part of this book to you. The jogging was neat because I ran along a trail I rarely used. I heard the birds sing; I smelled the forest. Trail work was more of an adventure. I trimmed the edges and cleaned several water bars. However, while doing that work, I noticed a huge tree branch which had fallen across the trail, forcing any traveler to duck under it order to proceed. So I got two small handsaws from the trail maintenance toolbox. One saw got stuck in the branch, however I had to use the other one to make a wedge to free the first one. Moreover, after much sweat and toil, I sawed through the offending branch and opened the trail. I felt successful. I completed my activities by writing one of this book's chapters. So I could chalk up two accomplishments—jogging and trail work—and they provided me with material for this book.

The first two activities satisfied my need for exercise, to be active, to be productive and make a good move, while the third fulfilled my mission to write this book. I almost just hurt myself right now. How? Trying to pat myself on my back, the reason for my joy was that I had walked the talk. Not only does this show an example of doing immediate and smaller projects, but it also demonstrates how small undertakings can enhance your big-picture goal.

Conclusion

Well, gang, what can we conclude about the big picture? And before addressing that, I must confess, I rambled bit more than usual in this chapter. How and why? The first answer is that this chapter differs from the five prior ones in that it does not feature dichotomies, but rather, it focuses on a central concept and its accompanying temporal sequences. Instead of the contradictory forms of the first five chapters, this one looks at complimentary aspects of the big picture and your everyday life. The second answer is that the Big Picture leads to a number of positive consequences. Having a goal allows one to pursue it immediately, such as climbing a mountain. However, there are also good results even when a major objective not immediately obtainable. These permits one to undertake activities and good moves, which will ultimately lead to your mission. Furthermore, I looked at the advantages of doing several activities simultaneously, such as jogging and talking together. I examined the innate power of just having a definite goal, alone because it gives you a perspective of what is important in your life and allows you to be perseverant enough to pursue it. Finally, the reflections on convergence and divergence as well as the discussion of strategy and tactics are just facets of the big picture and everyday life.

So here is the bottom line, having a big picture, major goals, missions, and a vision in your life are key and great. They also allow other activities to fit into a pattern which gives context to your world.

References

Edison, T, https://quoteinvestigator.com/2012/12/14/genius-ratio, 4/4/18.

LeBoeuf, M, https://www.brainyquote.com/quotes/michael_leboeuf_158247. 4/3/18.

Rodgers and Hammerstein, http://www.lyricsfreak.com/r/rodgers+and+hammerstein/climb+every+mountain_20599119.html. 4/2/18.

Tzu, S, https://www.davidbrim.com/sun-tzu-lessons-on-strategy. 4/3/18.

Witter, D, https://www.trademarkia.com/we-measure-success-one-investor-at-a-time-75603705.html 4/3/18.

CHAPTER 7

Transcendence

Pawtuckaway Lake

"Awe is an intuition for the dignity of all things, a realization that things not only are what they are but also stand, however remotely, for something supreme. Awe is a sense for transcendence, for the reference everywhere to mystery beyond all things."

—Rabbi Abraham Joshua Heschel

Westley and Foster and others, we have reached the final or the last chapter—either name sounds both intriguing and ominous. There is an old adage, "Saving the best for last." Well, perhaps this is true here. This chapter's idea basically challenges all I have said before. Up until now, I have dwelled in the land of dichotomies—following the rules or breaking them them, and the heart versus the head. Now, we enter the realm of the mysterious.

Moreover, these six chapters, although they represent a nice organizing point, do not fully tell the whole story. Here is why. Life is more confusing and complicated than just six contradictions. To illustrate, the United States' Supreme Court and other courts must make decisions. That is their job. But often, they are not picking between what is right and wrong. Rather they must decide between two rights. For example, they are weighing between property rights and one of the Bill of Rights. Yes, my grandsons, many things are easy or straightforward. Are they? But as your father is fond of saying, "Nothing is easy." So it has been said for every complicated, sophisticated problem, there is one simple direct answer. Reader take a deep breath and a pause. And that answer is wrong. This chapter advances transcendent solutions to life's dueling dualities.

Let me start with an example and an explanation of how this chapter came about. It was Wednesday, August 2010. And please note, as I keep telling you, I have been working on this book since before you were born. I had already worked out on the elliptical machine today because it was raining when I would have done my morning jog. Then the sun came out, and I so wanted to jog! My head said you have done your exercise for that day. My heart said enough for the day. But my spirit said jog. So my feet hit the pavement and I ran. At that moment, I discovered transcendence. It was neither head nor heart, it was just jogging!

Here is another example. This is to be read aloud to the tune of "It Was the Night before Christmas." It was the day after Christmas and two days after the first night of Hanukkah. When all through the house, and not a creature was stirring. The children were watching their Netflix program, and Peggy was busily engaged in the kitchen. I am left alone and wishing to join neither and certainly not to make such a clatter. I was bored. I prefer to be active. I have already exercised, and we have had our doubles in cribbage tournament against her children. Peggy and I won. What to do? I have already done an array of Internet games—hearts, cribbage, and pyramid solitaire. I won half of them. I did neither work on the big picture nor undertake a more immediate project. So I just played more computer games. It was another transcendent solution.

In both examples, I transcended the planned, prepared, and seemingly right thing to do. There were really no rules to follow or break.

Let us look at a variation of the transcendence theme. To do so, I will invoke an old chestnut: "Don't forget to smell the roses." All too often, in our hectic lives, we bypass or hurry through beauty and actually do not take the time to smell the roses or simply observe God's wonderful world. In the rush for *carpe diem,* we may seize the day but miss the seconds, minutes, and hours of it! Right at this moment, I am looking out over a calm, tranquil Pawtuckaway Lake, with its dramatic reflection of the magnificent late fall foliage. So I am practicing what I preach—I am writing to you and smelling the roses. I experienced the moment.

Let me try it yet another way. I live with a marvelous woman, Peggy Tucker. I am in love with her. But she breaks all my rules— she is not Jewish; she eats shrimp! She goes to church. She is sometimes not logical, but she is wonderful. You were warned about this in Chapter 3—The Heart Versus the Head. Love breaks the rules, makes new rules. And the new rules rule the day.

In closing this book, I am reminded of a poem a gentleman, whose name sadly I do not recall, wrote, "On a rock far out to sea, carved these words: 'Remember me.'"

It is my hope that these ideas proved helpful to you and others and that you remember me.

References

Abraham Joshua Heschel, *Who is man?'* 1965 Stanford University Press (CA)

Pawtuckaway Lake

My 'front lawn', Pawtuckaway Lake in the fall

It took a lifetime and a village to write this book. The following people, experiences and events have shaped my perspectives and have led to the creation of this book. My parents and sister have been the foundation of my life as stated in the volume's dedication. My life's partner, Peggy Tucker whose sharing, acceptance and demonstration of unconditional love speaks volumes and made this volume possible. My four children—Sasha, Ben, Matana and Barak—who are uniquely inspiring and proving that not only can you not predict what your kids will become but also you cannot predict what they will teach you. Two of whom have fantastic and talented spouses, Ben with Heather and Matana with Daniel. And they have all been uplifting to me. My two grandsons, Westley and Foster, to whom this book was written, have boundless energy and creativity. My co-authors of many articles and books—Foad Afshar, Patricia Bazemore, Robert Cadigan, Pam Kelly, Rabbi Peter Levy, Mary Ann McDuffee, Gary Moak, George McNeil, Marcy McWilliams, and David Siddle. My co-editor, Kyra Salancy, of the Appalachian Mountain Club 's *The Volunteer Exchange*, which brings the volunteers and the mountains together. Lucy Edwards and Elizabeth Bulkley whose editing has advanced my journalism. Gail Barton thanks for a lifetime of support. My work with Douglas Volk. My jogging and hiking buddies who have sustained me on the trail and provided for me lessons in perseverance and patience—Nick Bartol, Joe Donovan. Gordon Dubois, John Iwuc, Don Rice, David Riese, and Carl Schmottach. Albert Ullman who introduced me to sociology. James Hume who gave me my love of geology and showed me how rocks tell time. My Page Editors and Karla Varee who made sense out of my sentences and made it so that the pages speak volumes. My thanks to all of you. You all have provided the insights which have made this book possible.

Steve with Westley and Foster

ABOUT THE AUTHOR

Stephen Soreff, MD, is a retired psychiatrist, a diplomat in psychiatry, American Board of Psychiatry and Neurology. He has written, coauthored, and edited ten books, as well as many journal articles. The book titles include *Handbook for the Treatment of the Seriously Mentally Ill, Management of the Psychiatric Emergency, The Documentation Survival Handbook for Psychiatrists and Other Mental Health Professionals, E.M.S. Street Strategies: Effective Patient Interactions, Second Edition,* and *A Caregiver's Guide to Working with Combative Residents.* He has taught at Daniel Webster College, Southern New Hampshire University, Chester College of New England, Boston University, and New England College. He is the president of Education Initiatives LLC. http://eduinitiatives.com. Email info@eduinitiatives.com

He lives with his partner, Peggy Tucker, on the shores of Pawtuckaway Lake in New Hampshire. He has four fantastic children and two terrific grandchildren. He enjoys kayaking, hiking, jogging, learning Tai Chi and playing golf and pickle ball. He wants to be a stand-up comedian and is trying to reclimb all New Hampshire's forty-eight four-thousand-footer mountains.

CPSIA information can be obtained
at www.ICGtesting.com
Printed in the USA
LVHW020950291020
670026LV00007B/272

9 781645 448976